BURGUNDY STEW

BURGUNDY STEW

PETER MCINTOSH

CONTENTS

First Printing, 2025

ISBN 979-8-89686-425-7

CHAPTER ONE

Prologue

B rent Pineridge had always been different, even as a toddler. From his earliest days, his parents had noticed something off about him, though they couldn't quite put their finger on it. Unlike other babies who giggled at funny faces or reached out eagerly for toys, Brent's gaze would linger a moment too long on the faces around him, as though he were studying them. He rarely cried, even when he fell or was hungry, and his silence unnerved those who spent time around him.

His parents, Sandra and Neil initially dismissed these oddities as quirks of an introverted child. But as Brent grew older, their suspicions began to solidify into something closer to dread. His interests, his reactions, or lack thereof and even the way he played on his own seemed far from typical.

The strained and abusive relationship between Sandra and Neil did nothing to help Brent's development. Neil, a man prone to violent outbursts and harsh words, often directed his anger toward Sandra in front of their son. Sandra tried her best to shield Brent from the worst of it, but the tension in the household was palpable, permeating every corner of their modest home. He showed little interest in the friendships or games that excited other children his age.

Birthday parties were torture for him, the noise
and chaos causing him to retreat into a corner
with a book or, worse, to quietly leave without
anyone noticing.
Other kids didn't understand him,
and neither did their parents,
who whispered about Sandra's "odd boy"
behind her back.

By the time Brent reached school age, his reputation
as a quiet, withdrawn child had solidified.
Teachers described him as "bright but distant,"
someone who excelled academically but avoided
eye contact and group activities. He spent recess alone,
drawing or observing the other children with an
intensity that made some of them uneasy.

The few times he did engage with his peers,
his behaviour was peculiar, overly formal,
detached, and sometimes blunt.
It wasn't that Brent didn't understand emotions,
he simply seemed to lack them.
He could articulate how people felt
and even mimic the appropriate responses,
but there was no warmth behind his words or actions.
It was as if he were playing a role in a script
that he didn't truly believe in.

As the years passed, Brent's isolation deepened.
Sandra worried constantly about her son.
She longed for him to have a friend,

someone to pull him out of his shell
and show him the joys of connection.
But Brent seemed content in his solitude,
immersing himself in books, puzzles,
and, more disturbingly, an increasing
fascination with animals.
At first, Sandra was glad that Brent had found
a passion.
He spent hours sketching birds, rabbits, and foxes,
and his talent for detail was remarkable.
But there was something disconcerting
about the way he studied them,
as though they were specimens rather than
living creatures.

CHAPTER TWO

Early days

Brent had what appeared to be a normal upbringing
for an English boy.
He lived in a modest home with his father and mother, Sandra,
who doted on him with the kind of care and love
one might expect from a single parent.

Their home was situated in a quiet neighbourhood
filled with rows of similar houses,
where children played in the streets after school,
and elderly neighbours could often be seen tending
their gardens. On the surface, it was an idyllic community,
but there was something undeniably odd
about the area—specifically related to its pets.

Over the past year, a very large number of cats
and a few dogs had gone missing without a trace.
Owners who had once been greeted by the sound
of happy purring or wagging tails
were instead met with silence and
an unnerving sense of loss.
Flyers had been plastered on lampposts
and community noticeboards,
pleading for information,

but the animals seemed to have vanished into thin air.
Adding to the mystery,
the local animal shelter had reported a surprisingly
low number of rescues.
Usually, strays and lost pets would find their way there,
but recently, their kennels and cages remained
eerily empty.
Speculation ran rampant among the residents.
Some blamed foxes, others whispered about sinister
individuals lurking in the shadows.
Nobody could quite work out where these animals were going,
but the unease hung over the neighbourhood like a dark cloud.

Brent, however, seemed largely unaffected
by the strange happenings.
He was a quiet, introspective boy who preferred
books and solitary games to the noisy camaraderie
of playground antics.
At school, he was neither popular nor particularly disliked,
he simply existed on the periphery,
unnoticed by most.
He didn't often have friends over—or friends at all,
for that matter.
His mother had tried to encourage him to be more social,
but Brent seemed content in his solitude.
That was why it came as a surprise when he mentioned that
a schoolmate named Lewis would be coming over
after school for a play-date.
Sandra was thrilled. The idea of her son spending time
with a friend filled her with hope.
Maybe this was the start of Brent coming out of his shell,
she thought. She went all out to make the occasion special,
preparing a spread of snacks that could rival a birthday party

and tidying the house until it was spotless.

When the boys arrived, she greeted them with a wide smile
and an energy that bordered on overbearing.
She offered them plates of cookies, glasses of lemonade,
and a seemingly endless stream of suggestions
for activities they could do together.
The two boys, however, found her enthusiasm a little much.
Lewis, a wiry boy with freckles and an easy smile,
exchanged amused glances with Brent,
who shrugged as if to say, "That's just my mum."
Still, they settled into an awkward sort of camaraderie,
playing video games in the living room
while Sandra hovered nearby, trying to stifle her urge to
check on them every five minutes.

For a while, everything seemed to be going well.
The boys laughed at the ridiculous antics
in the game they were playing, their earlier awkwardness
melting away. Sandra watched from the kitchen,
her heart swelling with happiness.
It was a rare sight to see Brent so engaged
with someone his own age.
But things didn't continue going well.

As Sandra busied herself preparing
a fresh batch of snacks,
she heard a sudden commotion upstairs.
There was a series of loud, frantic thuds,
followed by a sickening crash.
The sound echoed through the house, and Sandra froze,
her heart pounding in her chest.
She rushed out of the kitchen,

her mind racing with fear and confusion.
When she reached the bottom of the staircase,
the sight before her made her stomach lurch.

Lewis was lying face down on the floor, motionless.
A massive pool of blood was spreading out from beneath him,
the dark red liquid seeping into
the cracks of the wooden floorboards.
Sandra let out a gasp, her hand flying to her mouth.
For a moment, she stood there,
paralysed by the horror of what she was seeing.
"Lewis!" she cried, rushing to his side.
She knelt, her hands trembling as she reached out
to check for signs of life.
His body was limp, and the warmth was already
starting to fade from his skin.
The injuries he had sustained were far worse
than what she would have expected from a
simple fall down the stairs.

His head was twisted at an unnatural angle,
and there was a deep gash on his temple that
was bleeding profusely.
Sandra looked up, her eyes searching for Brent.
He was standing at the top of the stairs,
his face expressionless.

There was something unsettling about the way
he was just standing there, staring down at the scene
without any visible emotion.
For a moment, their eyes met,
and Sandra felt a chill run down her spine.
"Brent, what happened?" she demanded, her voice shaky.

Brent didn't respond. He simply looked at her,
his gaze blank and unreadable.
Then, without a word, he turned
and disappeared into his bedroom,
closing the door behind him.

Sandra stared after him, her mind racing
with a thousand questions.
What had just happened? How could this have happened?
Frantic, she stumbled to the phone and dialled emergency services.
Her hands were trembling so badly that she could barely
press the buttons.
When the operator answered, she struggled
to explain the situation,
her words coming out in a panicked jumble.
The dispatcher assured her that help was on the way
and urged her to stay on the line until they arrived.
Minutes later, the paramedics arrived at the scene.
Sandra watched in a daze as they assessed Lewis's body,
their grim expressions confirming what she already knew.
The boy was dead. The police were called,
and soon the house was swarming with officers,
their questions relentless and probing.
Sandra tried her best to answer,
but her mind was a fog of grief and confusion.

Brent, meanwhile, remained in his room.
When the police questioned him,
his answers were vague and unhelpful.
He claimed not to remember what had happened,
saying only that Lewis had been running up and down
the stairs before he fell.
The officers exchanged sceptical glances but found

no evidence to contradict his story.
There were no signs of a struggle,
no witnesses to suggest foul play.
In the end, the incident was ruled a tragic accident,
and the case was closed.

But Sandra couldn't shake the feeling
that there was more to the story.
In the days and weeks that followed,
she found herself replaying the events
of that afternoon over and over in her mind.
Brent's strange behaviour,
the expression on his face as he stood at the top of the stairs,
the eerie stillness in his eyes,
it all felt wrong.
She noticed other things, too. Small,
unsettling details that she had previously overlooked.
For one, Brent had always been fascinated by animals.
He would spend hours watching nature documentaries
and sketching pictures of wildlife in his notebook.
But Sandra realised that his interest had taken
a darker turn in recent months.
She had found dead birds in the garden
on more than one occasion,
their necks twisted, or their bodies mutilated.
Brent had brushed it off,
claiming they must have been killed by a stray cat or a fox.
At the time, she had believed him. Now, she wasn't so sure.

Then there were the missing pets.
Sandra had dismissed the rumours as neighbourhood gossip,
but now she couldn't help but wonder.
Could Brent have had something to do with it?

The thought was almost too terrible to consider,
but it gnawed at her, refusing to be ignored.
As the days turned into weeks, Sandra's unease grew.
She began to watch Brent more closely,
studying his behaviour for any signs of guilt or remorse.
But he remained as quiet and inscrutable as ever,
his expression betraying nothing.
He continued to go to school, to read his books,
to draw in his notebook.
On the surface, everything seemed normal.
But Sandra couldn't shake the feeling
that something was deeply, fundamentally wrong.

CHAPTER THREE

Discovered

It was one of those unseasonably warm autumn afternoons,
the kind that begged for adventure.
A group of three boys had decided to explore
the dense forest that bordered their neighbourhood.
The forest had always been a source of both fascination
and fear for the local kids.
Parents warned them not to wander too far,
spinning tales of dangerous animals
and hidden sinkholes,
but these warnings only served to heighten the allure.
Today, curiosity got the better of them.

The forest was quieter than usual.
Typically, the chirping of birds and the rustling
of small animals in the underbrush provided
a comforting soundtrack to their escapades,
but today, an eerie stillness hung in the air.
The boys trudged through the undergrowth,
 their voices the only sound breaking the silence.
"Let's see how far we can go this time," said Kyle,
the de facto leader of the group.
He was the oldest and the bravest,
always the first to suggest climbing a tree

or crossing a stream.
The other two boys, Sam and Eric,
exchanged nervous glances but didn't protest.
None of them wanted to be the one
to suggest turning back.
After nearly an hour of wandering,
they stumbled upon something unexpected,
a clearing in the forest.
The boys stopped in their tracks,
their eyes widening as they took in the scene.
The clearing was surrounded
by thick brush and towering trees,
as if nature itself had tried to hide it.
But what lay within the clearing was
far from natural.

Someone had built a crude shelter in the centre.
It was made from branches and tarpaulin,
haphazardly tied together to form a sort of lean-to.
Inside, there was a makeshift table fashioned
from a plank of wood balanced on two tree stumps.
On the table were rusty knives, a pair of pliers,
and what looked like a bloodstained apron.
The sight sent a shiver down Kyle's spine,
but he said nothing.
"Who would live out here?"
Sam whispered his voice barely audible.
"Maybe it's a hunter,"
Kyle suggested, though his tone lacked conviction.
He stepped closer to the table,
his curiosity outweighing his fear.
The others hung back, watching him with a mix of
admiration and trepidation.

Nearby, several rectangular patches of ground
had been disturbed.
The soil was loose and uneven, as if someone had recently
dug and then hastily filled them back in.
Eric crouched down beside one of the patches,
running his fingers through the dirt.
"Why would someone dig holes here?"
he asked, looking up at the others.
Eric voiced what he was thinking. "They're graves."
The boys stared at him,
their expressions a mix of disbelief and unease.
"What do you mean?" Kyle asked, his bravado faltering.
Eric gestured toward the patches of soil.
"They're the right size for small animals.
Cats, maybe dogs.
Someone's been burying them here."
A heavy silence fell over the group
as the weight of his words sank in.
The missing pets. The flyers on lamp posts.
The empty animal shelter.
It all seemed to point to this place.

"Let's get out of here," Sam said, his voice trembling.
He backed away from the clearing,
his eyes darting around as if expecting someone,
or something to appear from the shadows.
But Kyle wasn't ready to leave.
He moved toward the shelter, his eyes fixed on the table.
"We should look around more," he said.
"Maybe we can figure out who did this."
"No way," Eric said. "This is messed up.
What if they come back?"

"They're not here now," Kyle argued.
He picked up one of the knives from the table,
examining it closely.
"Look at this. There's dried blood on it.
Whoever has been here,
they've been doing...something."

Eric's gaze wandered to the campfire pit nearby.
It was surrounded by blackened stones,
and the ashes within were still faintly warm.
He crouched down and poked at the remnants with a stick,
uncovering fragments of charred bones.
"Look," he said, holding up one of the pieces.
"They've been cooking them."
Sam gagged, turning away in horror.
Eric's face went pale, and even Kyle seemed to lose his nerve.
"Okay, we're leaving," Kyle said,
dropping the knife as if it had burned him. "Now."

The boys turned and hurried back the way they had come,
their earlier sense of adventure
replaced by a growing sense of dread.
As they pushed through the undergrowth,
the silence of the forest seemed to press in on them,
amplifying the sound of their own footsteps and ragged breathing.
Eric lagged, his mind racing.
The scene in the clearing had disturbed him, yes,
but it had also fascinated him.
There was a strange, almost magnetic pull to the place,
a sense that it held secrets waiting to be uncovered.
He glanced over his shoulder one last time,
his eyes lingering on the shelter until it disappeared.
When they finally emerged from the forest,

the boys parted ways without a word.
Each of them carried the weight of what they had seen,
unsure of how to process it.

As Eric walked home alone,
his thoughts a whirlwind of images and questions.
Who had built the shelter?
Why were they burying animals in the forest?
And, most importantly, what did it all mean?
That night, as he lay in bed,
Eric couldn't shake the feeling that the clearing
was connected to the strange events in the neighbourhood.
The missing pets, the whispers of foxes and predators,
it all seemed too convenient.
He stared at the ceiling, his mind replaying
the scene over and over.
He knew he had to go back.
There was something about that place,
something he needed to understand.

The next morning, Eric woke before dawn.
He dressed quickly and slipped out of the house,
careful not to wake his family.
The streets were deserted, the world still shrouded
in the dim light of early morning.
He made his way to the edge of the forest,
his heart pounding with a mixture of fear and anticipation.
When he reached the clearing,
the sight that greeted him stopped him in his tracks.
The shelter was gone. The table, the knives,
the campfire—they had all disappeared.
Even the disturbed patches of soil
had been smoothed over,

as if nothing had ever been there.
Eric stood there, his mind reeling.
Someone had been here,
erasing all traces of their presence.
But as he turned to leave, something caught his eye.
Lying at the edge of the clearing was a small,
bloodstained collar.
Eric picked it up, turning it over in his hands.
Eric stuffed the collar into his pocket
and hurried back home, his mind racing.
Whoever was responsible for the clearing
hadn't just been burying pets,
they had been killing them.
And now, they knew someone had found their secret.

CHAPTER FOUR

Moving away

Arguments between Brent's mother and father became
increasingly heated, filling the house with a tension
so thick it seemed to seep into the walls.
Plates clattered, doors slammed,
and voices were raised in a crescendo of anger
that often ended in silence,
a silence heavier than the shouting had been.

Brent would retreat to his room,
pressing a pillow over his ears,
trying to block out the storm outside.
But even the thickest walls couldn't shield him from
the reverberations of their fights.
They had begun to creep into every corner of his life,
shadowing him at school and making his chest tighten
every time he walked through the front door.

His father's violent outbursts only made matters worse.
A missed chore or a stray look was enough to provoke a reaction,
leaving Brent reeling for days.
His arms bore the quiet testament of bruises that
he tried to hide under long sleeves,
even in the sweltering heat of summer.

The physical pain was sharp and fleeting,
but it was the emotional scars that lingered,
a deep-seated fear and distrust that burrowed into his soul.

Some mornings, the weight of it all was too much.
Brent would lie in bed, staring at the ceiling,
unable to summon the strength to face another day.
Weeks would pass without him setting foot in a classroom.
The school sent letters, and his mother made excuses,
but everyone seemed to know what was going on
without ever addressing it directly.

Finally, the day came when his parents decided
they couldn't go on together.
The split was inevitable, yet it still felt sudden.
Brent's mother, worn thin from years of trying
to hold everything together,
made the difficult decision to send him to live
with his grandmother.
It was a move born of love and desperation,
a hope that a change of environment might offer
him the stability he so desperately needed.

Brent arrived at his grandmother's house with
a single suitcase and a heart full of apprehension.
The house was small, with walls painted in warm hues
and a garden bursting with colourful flowers.
His grandmother, a petite woman with silver hair
and a ready smile, greeted him with open arms.
Her hugs were firm and reassuring,
a stark contrast to the world he had left behind.
"Welcome home, Brent," she said,
her voice soft and soothing.

"We'll make it work, together."
At first, Brent kept to himself.
He spent hours in his room,
unpacking and rearranging his things,
or sitting by the window, watching the world go by.

His grandmother, sensing his need for space,
didn't push. Instead,
she left small gestures of care:
a plate of cookies on his desk, fresh sheets on his bed,
and a steady stream of quiet encouragement.
The new school was another source of anxiety.
Brent had always been a loner,
and the idea of starting over in a place
where he knew no one was daunting.
But from the moment he walked through the gates,
he noticed a difference.
The teachers were patient and understanding,
and the students were surprisingly kind.
They didn't press him with too many questions
or make him feel out of place.
Instead, they welcomed him with small acts
of inclusion,
a shared lunch, an invitation to join a game,
or a simple "hey" in the hallway.

Over the next few weeks,
Brent began to settle into a routine.
Mornings started with the smell of
freshly brewed coffee and the sound of birds chirping
outside his window.
His grandmother would wave him off to school
with a cheerful "Have a good day!"

and a packed lunch in hand.
At school, he found himself opening up,
little by little.
He started participating in class,
answering questions,
and even making a few tentative jokes
that earned him smiles and laughter
from his classmates.

It was a slow process, but the changes were unmistakable.
Brent's resting expression,
once a mask of guarded mistrust, began to soften.
His eyes, previously dull and downcast,
now held a glimmer of curiosity.
He still preferred solitude,
but there was a warmth to his demeanour
that hadn't been there before.
For the first time in a long time,
he felt a sense of safety and belonging.

One afternoon, as he walked home from school,
Brent noticed a stray dog limping along the side of the road.
The dog's fur was matted,
and its ribs were visible through its thin frame.
Without thinking,
Brent crouched down and extended a hand.
The dog hesitated, its tail wagging nervously,
before inching closer.
Brent smiled for what felt like the first time in years.
"Hey there, buddy," he said softly.
"Looks like you've had a rough time too."
He coaxed the dog into following him home,
where his grandmother helped him clean and feed it.

They named the dog Lucky,
and it quickly became a fixture in their lives.
Lucky's playful antics brought laughter into the house,
and Brent found solace in the unconditional love
of his new companion.

As the weeks turned into months, Brent continued to heal.
He joined the school's art club,
where he discovered a talent for drawing.
His sketches, initially dark and brooding,
began to reflect the world around him:
the vibrant flowers in his grandmother's garden,
the smiling faces of his classmates,
and the wagging tail of Lucky.
Each stroke of the pencil was a step toward
reclaiming his sense of self.
One evening, as he and his grandmother sat outdoors,
watching the sunset,
she turned to him and said, "You know, Brent,
you're stronger than you realise.
You've been through so much but look at you now.
You're growing into someone kind, someone who cares."
Brent didn't know how to respond.
He simply nodded, his throat tight with emotion.
Her words stayed with him, though,
echoing in his mind long after the sun had set.
Life wasn't perfect, and there were still moments
when the past threatened to pull him under.
But Brent had found a new foundation,
one built on kindness, resilience,
and the quiet strength of his grandmother's love.
For the first time in his life, he dared to hope for a brighter future.

CHAPTER FIVE

Goodbye to school

B rent's life had turned in ways no one, not even he,
could have foreseen. Only a few years earlier,
he had been the quiet, withdrawn boy whose presence
in the classroom was barely acknowledged.
His grades had become dismal, his social life non-existent,
and his future looked as bleak as the dark clouds he often
stared at through the window.
But now, as he stood at the threshold
of his final year of school,
Brent was a young man transformed.

The change had not been easy or swift,
but it had been profound.
And at the heart of that transformation
was his grandmother, Eleanor.
Eleanor had stepped in when Brent's life
was at its lowest point.
His parents, caught in their own struggles,
had vanished out of his life,
leaving him to fend for himself.
It was Eleanor who took him into her
modest but warm home,
a small cottage with a neatly kept garden

and an old oak tree that provided shade in the summer.
At first, Brent had resisted her efforts to reach him.
He carried his hurt like armour,
his resentment toward his parents
spilling over onto anyone who tried to help.
But Eleanor was patient.
She didn't push or prod; instead,
she created an environment where Brent could begin to heal.

Every evening, they sat down to dinner together,
a ritual Brent hadn't experienced in years.
The meals were simple but delicious,
often accompanied by Eleanor's stories
about her own childhood.
Brent would listen silently at first, but over time,
he began to share his own thoughts and memories.
Those dinners became a cornerstone of their relationship,
a place where trust and understanding slowly grew.

Eleanor's influence extended far beyond the dinner table.
She introduced Brent to the local library,
a place she had frequented since her youth.
At first, Brent had little interest in the shelves of books
that stretched endlessly before him.
But Eleanor had a way of making things seem inviting
rather than mandatory.
She would leave books lying around the house,
mysteries, adventure novels, even graphic novels,
knowing Brent's curiosity would
eventually get the better of him.

One rainy afternoon, Brent picked up a battered copy
of *The Hobbit* from the coffee table.

By the time Eleanor returned from the garden,
drenched from pulling weeds in the drizzle,
Brent was halfway through the first chapter.
From that moment, reading became an escape for him,
a way to explore worlds far beyond the confines
of his own troubled life.

It wasn't long before Brent began creating his own stories.
He filled notebooks with characters, plots,
and fantastical settings.
Eleanor discovered one of these notebooks
by accident and was astonished by his talent.
"You have a gift," she told him.
"You should share this with others."
At her urging, Brent showed a story to his English teacher,
Mrs. Carter, who was equally impressed.
Mrs. Carter read it aloud to the class, her voice bringing
Brent's words to life.
When the story ended, the room erupted in applause.
For the first time, Brent felt truly seen,
not as a failure or a problem,
but as someone with potential.
Encouraged by Eleanor and Mrs. Carter,
Brent began to excel in school.
His grades, once abysmal, steadily improved.
He started participating in class discussions
and even joined the drama club,
where he discovered a flair for improvisation and comedy.
Onstage, he could be anyone he wanted to be,
and the laughter and applause from the audience
became a new kind of validation.

But Eleanor's support wasn't limited to academics.

She taught Brent about life,
the importance of kindness,
the value of hard work,
and the strength it took to forgive.
She shared stories of her own struggles,
how she had overcome loss and disappointment,
and how those experiences had shaped
her into the person she was.
"Life isn't about avoiding storms," she would say,
"but about learning to dance in the rain."
Brent took those lessons to heart.
He began helping Eleanor around the house,
mowing the lawn, repairing the old fence,
and even planting flowers in the garden.
He volunteered to tutor younger students at school,
earning their admiration and respect.
He found joy in making others laugh,
in being a source of positivity rather than a burden.

Yet, despite all the progress he had made,
there was one part of Brent's life
that remained unresolved: his parents.
Their absence loomed over him like a shadow,
a constant reminder of the pain he had endured.
Eleanor never pressured him to talk about them,
but she was always there when he needed to.
"I don't understand how they could just abandon me,"
Brent said one evening as they sat outdoors,
watching the sun set over the horizon.
Eleanor placed a hand on his shoulder.
"People make mistakes, Brent.
Sometimes big ones.
But their mistakes don't define you.

You're so much more than what's happened to you."
Those words stayed with Brent, giving him the strength
to focus on the future rather than the past.
As graduation approached, he began to dream about what lay ahead.

His teachers encouraged him to apply for scholarships,
convinced he had the talent and determination
to succeed in college.
His friends talked excitedly about their plans
for the summer and beyond,
including a road trip Brent had been invited to join.
On the night of his graduation,
the school gymnasium was packed with students,
teachers, and proud families.
Brent scanned the crowd until he found Eleanor,
sitting near the front, her smile as radiant as the sun.
When his name was called, and he walked across the stage
to receive his diploma, the applause was deafening.

Later that evening, they celebrated at home
with a simple but heartfelt meal.
Eleanor had baked a cake, her icing a little uneven
but delicious, nonetheless.
"To new beginnings," she said, raising her glass
of sparkling cider.
"To new beginnings," Brent echoed,
his heart full of gratitude.
As they sat outdoors afterwards,
the stars twinkling above them,
Brent felt a sense of peace he hadn't known in years.
He didn't know exactly what the future held,
but he knew one thing for certain,
with Eleanor's love and support,

he was ready to face whatever came next.

CHAPTER SIX

Hard work

B rent's graduation had been a proud moment for both him
and his grandmother, Eleanor.
But once the celebratory glow faded, reality set in.
The question of what came next loomed large.
Brent's teachers had encouraged him to apply
for university scholarships,
but he struggled with the idea of accepting what felt like charity.
Brent wasn't interested in handouts, he wanted to earn his own way.
With no money for tuition and no clear path forward,
Brent made the decision to step into the workforce.

After scouring the classifieds and knocking on countless doors,
he landed a job at a small, family-run restaurant
on the edge of town.
The restaurant, *Delilah's Kitchen*, wasn't anything fancy,
but its atmosphere and loyal clientele
made it a community staple.
Brent's role was far from glamorous.
As a kitchen porter,
he was responsible for the most mundane and menial tasks.
His days were filled with chopping vegetables,
scrubbing pots, mopping floors,
and tackling mountains of dirty dishes.

He worked long hours for modest pay,
often leaving the kitchen drenched in sweat
and smelling of onions and grease.
But Brent approached the work
with a positive attitude that surprised even himself.

He thought often of his grandmother's advice:
"Hard work is never wasted.
Every task you do is a step toward something bigger."
Those words became his mantra.
At first, the other kitchen staff barely noticed him.
To them, he was just another teenager passing through,
a cog in the machine.
But Brent's diligence and upbeat demeanour
soon caught their attention.
He didn't complain, even when faced with the dirtiest jobs.
Instead, he focused on doing each task
as efficiently and thoroughly as possible.
It wasn't long before the head chef,
a gruff but fair man named Tony, began to take note.
"You've got a good work ethic, kid,"
Tony said one evening as Brent wiped down the counters
after a particularly hectic dinner rush.
"Stick around, and you might learn something."

Encouraged by the recognition,
Brent threw himself even more fully into his work.
He asked questions, observed the chefs as they prepared dishes,
and practised knife skills during his breaks.
Gradually, Tony began assigning him more responsibilities.
First, it was preparing garnishes and assembling salads.
Then, it was learning to season and marinate meats.
Before long, Brent was helping with sauces and side dishes,

his hands moving with growing confidence and precision.
As Brent's skills improved, so did his standing in the kitchen.
The tasks he had once done were delegated to newer hires,
and he found himself working alongside
the line cooks during busy shifts.
The camaraderie in the kitchen, once distant,
became a source of motivation.

Brent discovered that he enjoyed the fast-paced environment,
the adrenaline of service, and the satisfaction
of sending out plates he had helped create.
Over time, Brent became a valued member of the team.
Customers who peeked into the open kitchen
would often see him working diligently,
his brow furrowed in concentration
as he plated dishes or prepped ingredients.

The restaurant's owner, Delilah,
began to trust him with more responsibilities,
even asking for his input on new menu items.
But Brent's ambitions didn't stop
at becoming a good line cook.
While he enjoyed the work and appreciated
the opportunities he had been given,
he had a dream that quietly grew within him.
Inspired by the stories he had read as a teenager
and his newfound love of food,
Brent dreamed of opening a restaurant of his own,
one that would combine his passion for storytelling
with the culinary skills he was honing.
To make that dream a reality,
Brent knew he needed to save every penny he could.
Though his wages weren't high, he was disciplined in his spending.

He lived frugally, walking to work instead of taking the bus
and being careful to avoid unnecessary expenses.
He set aside a portion of all the money he earned,
watching his savings grow bit by bit.

Eleanor was his biggest cheerleader.
Though she worried about him working such long hours,
she admired his determination and focus.
"You've always been good at seeing the big picture,"
she told him one evening over tea. "Keep at it, and you'll get there."
As the years passed, Brent became an integral part
of *Delilah's Kitchen*.
He contributed to the restaurant's success in countless ways,
from refining its recipes to mentoring younger staff.
He learned every aspect of the business,
from managing inventory to balancing costs,
soaking up knowledge like a sponge.

But despite his growing role in the restaurant,
Brent never let his dream slip out of sight.
On his days off, he spent hours sketching out ideas
for his future venture.
He envisioned a place where each dish told a story,
where the menu was a journey through flavours and memories.
He even experimented in Eleanor's kitchen,
testing recipes and asking for her feedback.

One particularly quiet evening at the restaurant,
Tony pulled Brent aside.
"You've got talent, kid," he said,
his tone uncharacteristically soft.
"You could go places if you wanted to.
Ever thought about running your own kitchen?"

Brent hesitated for a moment, then nodded.
"Yeah, I have," he admitted.
Tony smiled.
"Good. Keep learning, keep saving,
and don't lose sight of what you want.
You've got what it takes."
Those words stayed with Brent, fuelling his resolve.
He continued to work tirelessly,
putting in extra hours when needed
and always striving to improve.

The restaurant became a second home to him,
a place where he could test his limits and grow.
By the time Brent reached his mid-twenties,
he had almost saved enough money
to take the first steps toward his dream.
Though he wasn't sure exactly
how or when he would open his own restaurant,
he knew he was closer than ever.
One evening, after closing the restaurant,
Brent sat with Delilah and Tony,
sharing a quiet drink to celebrate another successful week.
"You know," Delilah said, looking at Brent thoughtfully,
"when you first started here,
I didn't think you'd last a month.
But you've proven me wrong in every possible way."
Brent chuckled. "I've learned a lot here.
More than I ever thought I would."
"Well," Tony said, raising his glass,
"here's to what comes next.
Whatever it is, I know you'll make it great."

As Brent walked home that night,

the cool breeze carrying the scent of blooming jasmine,
he felt a sense of pride and anticipation.
He still had a long way to go,
but he was ready for the journey ahead.
With Eleanor's unwavering support,
the lessons he had learned at *Delilah's Kitchen*,
and his own determination,
Brent knew that the path he had chosen,
though unconventional,
was leading him toward something extraordinary.

CHAPTER SEVEN

Tragedy

The news came quietly,
    as though the universe had decided that
even the loudest of tragedies should fall on deaf ears.
Brent had always thought of his grandmother
as a force of nature,
an indomitable presence in his life.
She was the one who had shaped him, supported him,
and loved him unconditionally.
So when Eleanor passed away in her sleep,
it felt like the world had tilted on its axis,
throwing him into an abyss of grief and loss
that no amount of time could ever heal.

It had been a sudden decline. For months,
Eleanor had been battling a slow,
creeping illness that she had refused to acknowledge at first.
A few trips to the doctor, some medication, and a lot of "I'm fine"
had kept everyone, including Brent, at bay,
in denial.
But one cold winter morning,
Brent came downstairs to find her sitting quietly
in her favourite chair by the window,
the mug of tea she had always kept by her side now cold.

Her usual twinkle of life was gone from her eyes.
It was only then that Brent understood
 she was no longer the woman who had once been so full of life.
And he wasn't prepared for what would come next.

When the end finally came,
it was as if she had simply decided that her work was done.
Brent held her hand that final morning,
the same hand that had once steadied him when he was unsure,
the same hand that had guided him through years of hardship.
There were no final words, no dramatic gestures.
She just slipped away,
leaving behind a silence that Brent would never truly get used to.

The funeral was quiet, attended
by only a few of the people
Brent had come to know over the years.
The small, intimate service felt like
a strange reflection of the life Eleanor had lived,
a life of simplicity and quiet grace,
unassuming yet deeply impactful.
Brent stood by her grave,
the wind bitter and unforgiving,
and it felt like the cold seeped deep into his bones.
He realised then that this kind of loss was not something
you could ever truly prepare for.

The grief that followed was overwhelming.
Even the simplest tasks felt impossible.
For days, Brent wandered through the house
that had been his refuge,
now a hollow shell without the woman who had given it warmth.
The kitchen,

once filled with the comforting smells of Eleanor's cooking,
was now an empty space where memories lingered like ghosts.
Despite the emotional toll,
there was a practical side to the situation that Brent had to face.
Eleanor had left him the house and her life savings.
It wasn't much by most standards,
but it was enough to offer Brent a small cushion.
The house was worth something.
And the savings, while modest,
were enough to boost the money Brent had been putting
aside for years.

It wasn't much, but it was enough.
It was more than enough.
And with it, Brent had the means to pursue the dream
his grandmother had always believed in,
opening his own restaurant.
The idea had been in Brent's heart for years,
slowly taking shape as he worked alongside
the chefs and owners at *Delilah's Kitchen*.
Where he had honed his craft,
learned the ropes of the restaurant business,
and developed an unshakeable confidence in his abilities.
But the dream had always seemed just out of reach.
Without enough resources to make it happen,
it was something he tucked away in the corner of his mind,
like a treasure he couldn't afford to unearth.
But now, it seemed both the right
and the inevitable time to bring that dream to life.

Brent knew that opening a restaurant
would require more than just money,
it would take sweat, time, and every ounce of energy he had.

It was going to be a monumental challenge.
But if there was one thing his grandmother had taught him,
it was that hard work, no matter how difficult,
was always worth it.

The first step was finding a location.
Brent spent weeks scouting potential places,
looking at old buildings, new developments,
and vacant storefronts.
He needed a space that was affordable but had character,
a place that could be transformed into something unique.
He wanted the restaurant to have a story,
to reflect everything he had learned over the years,
the importance of simplicity, the beauty of food,
and the connection between a meal
and the people who shared it.

After a few months of searching, he found it,
a small, worn building on a busy street corner.
It wasn't much at first glance,
but Brent could see its potential.
The space was just big enough to accommodate
a modest dining area, a kitchen, and a small bar.
It was tucked away, but not too far off the beaten path.
It was perfect.

Brent took the plunge, using most of the money he had
to secure the lease and begin renovations.
He knew it wasn't going to be easy. Every penny counted,
and every decision had to be carefully considered.
He had no investors, no partners,
just enough money and a fierce determination.

The renovations were gruelling,
a constant push and pull of conflicting priorities.
There were days when Brent was so exhausted
he could barely think straight, but he pressed on,
sometimes working late into the night to finish tasks.
He picked out the paint colours, designed the logo,
and found the right equipment for the kitchen.
The place began to take shape, a warm,
inviting atmosphere with an open kitchen,
rustic wooden tables,
and dim lighting that gave the space an intimate,
almost magical feel.

As the weeks went on, Brent brought in a small team of staff.
He was selective,
looking for people who shared his vision and work ethic.
He knew that building a restaurant wasn't just about
cooking great food,
it was about creating an experience,
a place where people felt at home.
Slowly, the team began to come together,
waitstaff, cooks, dishwashers, and managers,
each contributing in their own way to the
creation of his dream.

The menu was Brent's pride and joy.
It was simple but sophisticated,
classic dishes with a modern twist,
 each plate carefully crafted to tell a story.
He poured his heart into every recipe,
drawing on his years of experience
and the lessons his grandmother had taught him.
Eleanor's influence was present in every aspect of the restaurant,

from the comforting flavours of her home cooking to the ethos of
hard work and humility she had instilled in him.

When the day finally came to open the doors,
Brent felt a mix of excitement and anxiety.
The restaurant was still a work in progress,
with little imperfections here and there.
But he had done it.
He had created something out of nothing,
just as he had promised
his grandmother he would.

The first few weeks were a blur.
The restaurant, named *Eleanor's*
in honour of the woman who had shaped his life,
was a hit. People came in to try the food,
drawn by word of mouth and the restaurant's warm,
inviting atmosphere.
Brent worked tirelessly,
overseeing every aspect of the operation, cooking,
managing, greeting customers,
and ensuring that everything ran smoothly.

Though the challenges of running a restaurant were immense,
Brent found a new sense of fulfilment that
he hadn't known before.
He wasn't just working for money anymore,
he was working to bring something
he had dreamed of to life.
And with each successful service, with each satisfied customer,
he felt his grandmother's presence guiding him,
as if she were watching over him and offering her quiet support.

But even with all the progress and success,
Brent knew he would never truly recover from losing Eleanor.
The pain of her absence was still a constant weight on his heart,
a reminder that the person who had shaped him,
who had believed in him when no one else did, was no longer there.
There were moments of quiet loneliness,
when the restaurant emptied out
and the staff went home for the night,
when Brent would sit alone in the kitchen,
reflecting on how far he had come.

He missed her. He missed her laugh, her quiet wisdom,
the way she could make everything seem okay.
But despite the pain, Brent knew that the restaurant
was more than just a tribute to her,
it was a living, breathing extension of everything she had taught him.
Eleanor's was more than just a business. It was a symbol of resilience,
of love, and of the power of hard work.
And with each passing day, Brent knew
he was honouring his grandmother
in the best way possible,
by continuing to pursue his dream, no matter how hard it got.

CHAPTER EIGHT

Missing

B rent had always considered himself lucky to live in such a
peaceful neighbourhood. The small, tree-lined street
where his grandmother had raised her family was a place
that felt rooted in tradition.
It was a safe, well-established community where people knew
each other's names, and children played freely
outside without fear.
The houses, though ageing gracefully,
had been carefully maintained and lovingly renovated by the
new generation of upper-middle-class families who had moved in.
The neighbourhood hadn't deteriorated as others had,
instead, it had matured, with a sense of pride in its history
and an eagerness to maintain its charm.

Brent's grandmother, Eleanor, had always spoken fondly
of the old days.
She had raised Brent's mother here.
Brent could see that the streets were filled with memories
and old friends, old houses, old routines.
It was a place where people knew each other
and looked out for one another.
Brent had also now grown up with
the comforting sense of stability

that only a neighbourhood like this could provide.

Crime was a rarity in this part of town.
A few break-ins here and there,
but nothing that ever made the news.
The police rarely had to patrol the area,
and most evenings were quiet,
the sound of crickets and distant laughter from family
gatherings drifting through the air.
For Brent, the neighbourhood was an oasis of calm,
a haven where nothing ever seemed to change.
But that all changed when the reports started coming in.

It began as a whisper—small talk between neighbours,
an exchange of worried glances in the grocery store.
People were disappearing. At first, it was just one or two
isolated incidents:
a young woman last seen walking home
from a late shift at the local diner,
a middle-aged man who had gone for an evening jog
and never returned.
These were tragic, no doubt,
but it was easy to dismiss them as mere coincidence,
as isolated events that could be explained away
by bad luck or unfortunate circumstances.

But then it started happening more frequently.
The cases began to pile up—month after month,
there was a new report of a missing person.
At first, it was only one or two people,
but soon it became a pattern.
And it wasn't just anyone.
It was people who lived in the same neighbourhood as Brent,

people he saw walking their dogs or going to work in the mornings.
It wasn't confined to one age group either—there were teenagers,
young professionals, middle-aged men and women.
There was no clear connection, no pattern that made sense.
They all simply disappeared, and no one had any answers.

The local news stations ran stories, but there were no clues.
No witnesses. No leads.
It was as if these people had simply vanished into thin air.
The police had no answers either.
They combed the area for evidence,
interviewed family members,
and scoured local CCTV footage,
but nothing turned up. It was like they had never existed.
The sense of unease that had begun to simmer
in the neighbourhood started to boil over.
People grew cautious,
locking their doors at night
and drawing the blinds a little tighter.
Neighbours who had once been friendly
and chatty were now more reserved,
avoiding eye contact when they passed on the sidewalk.
The neighbourhood had become a place of quiet suspicion,
especially at night.
Everyone was on edge, unsure of who could be trusted
and who was hiding something.

The common thread between the disappearances
was unsettling:
they all happened to people who were out walking alone at night.
There were no reports of anyone being abducted in broad daylight,
no confrontations or signs of violence.
But every person who went missing had been out alone,

typically on foot,
often during the late hours of the evening
when the neighbourhood was quiet and empty.
The woods at the edge of the neighbourhood,
which had always been a peaceful place for joggers
and dog walkers,
now seemed darker, more menacing.
The streets, once lined with old oak trees
and rows of well-kept homes,
now felt like a maze of shadows.

There was a marked increase
in the number of people who stayed indoors after dark.
People who had once been outside chatting with friends
were now inside.
More families were getting security cameras installed,
and there was a noticeable uptick
in the number of vehicles parked outside homes at night.
The police held town meetings,
trying to ease the public's growing anxiety.
They assured the residents
that they were doing everything they could to find
the culprits,
that they were investigating every angle.
They asked everyone to stay vigilant,
to report anything suspicious,
but the truth was that there was nothing concrete to report.
It was as though the missing people
were being swallowed by the night,
vanishing without a trace, as if they had simply stepped
out of one world and into another.

Brent started to hear whispers about theories.

Some believed it was the work of a serial kidnapper,
someone who was targeting vulnerable people late at night.
Others suggested it was something more supernatural,
an urban legend that had resurfaced.
It didn't help that the disappearances seemed
to happen during the darkest months of the year,
when the nights were long,
and the streets were often empty.
People began to speculate,
sharing stories of strange occurrences,
of fleeting figures seen in the shadows,
of lights flickering in empty houses.
Some even claimed to have heard strange noises
coming from the woods at night.

One evening, one of the frequent patrons from the restaurant
made his way home through the quiet streets.
As he walked past the park near the edge of the neighbourhood,
he felt the familiar chill in the air.
The wind rustled the leaves of the trees,
and the shadows seemed deeper, longer.
His footsteps echoed in the stillness,
and he couldn't shake the feeling that he wasn't alone.
He quickened his pace,
his mind racing with every creak of the branches overhead.
As he passed the park entrance,
he caught a glimpse of something,
a shadowy figure darting between the trees.
His heart skipped a beat, and instinctively, he turned to look.
But by the time he had fully turned, there was nothing there.
The park was empty, the night silent once again.
His pulse quickened as he continued home,
the unsettling feeling clinging to him

long after he had crossed the threshold of his house.
The hairs on the back of his neck stood on end,
and he realised with a sinking feeling that the fear
that had taken hold of the neighbourhood
had finally crept into his own life.
The streets that had once been so familiar, so safe,
now seemed like a labyrinth of uncertainty.
He locked the door behind him,
drew the curtains, and sat in silence for a long while.
He couldn't shake the thought that the disappearances
were more than just random occurrences,
that something dark and inexplicable was at work.

CHAPTER NINE

Success

It had been several years since Brent had opened *Eleanor's*,
and in those years, the restaurant had grown beyond
anything he had ever imagined.
What had started as a dream fuelled by his grandmother's
legacy had blossomed into a thriving establishment
with a loyal customer base.
There were nights when the restaurant
was packed to the brim,
and Brent couldn't help but stand back
and take in the bustling atmosphere,
the laughter, the clinking of glasses,
the hum of contented conversation.

His restaurant had become a fixture in the neighbourhood,
a place where people gathered to celebrate
birthdays, anniversaries, and the simple joy of a good meal.
The once small and unassuming *Eleanor's*
had transformed into a beloved institution,
known not just for its warm, welcoming ambiance,
but for the exquisite dishes that left people coming back for more.

Brent had surrounded himself with a talented team of chefs,
waitstaff, and managers,

all of whom shared his passion for food and customer service.
The kitchen had become a well-oiled machine,
each person performing their duties with precision and care.
The head chef, Marco, was an incredibly skilled cook,
and his assistants worked tirelessly to ensure that every dish
that left the kitchen was nothing short of perfect.

The restaurant ran smoothly, and Brent's days were spent
overseeing operations,
engaging with customers,
and ensuring that everything was in order.
But despite the large team and the many hands that worked
in the kitchen,
there was one dish that Brent kept entirely to himself.

The Burgundy Stew was the crown jewel of *Eleanor's*.
Described on the menu as a hearty,
comforting dish of slow-cooked meat in a rich red wine gravy,
served with a medley of vegetables,
it was a favourite among the regulars.
It was a dish that Brent had perfected over the years,
and it was the one thing he never allowed anyone else to prepare.
Marco, the head chef,
had asked more than once to assist in making it,
but Brent would always politely decline,
insisting that the Burgundy Stew was a dish
he preferred to handle himself.

It wasn't that Brent didn't trust Marco or his team,
it was more than that.
The Burgundy Stew was his creation,
his personal touch that had become a symbol of *Eleanor's* success.
It was a dish that had come to represent not just the food he served,

but the essence of the restaurant itself,
comfort, warmth, and a deep connection to his past.
Every time he made it,
it was like a tribute to his life, the good and the bad.

Brent had never shared the full details of the dish's recipe
with anyone—not even Marco.
There were things about the stew that only he knew,
small secrets that made it different from any other stew in town.
He was protective of those secrets,
and he had always felt that if anyone else were to cook it,
something essential would be lost.
There was an artistry to it,
a rhythm in the way the ingredients came together,
and Brent couldn't bear the thought of it being made
by anyone else.

The Burgundy Stew was a dish that required
patience, precision,
and a deep understanding of flavours.
Brent had spent years perfecting it, adjusting the seasoning,
testing different cuts of meat,
experimenting with the right kind of wine.
It was a labour of love, a dish that demanded attention
and time.
He would start preparing it in the early morning,
simmering the meat in the wine and broth for hours,
allowing the flavours to meld together.
The scent of the stew would fill the kitchen, warm and inviting,
as Brent added the final touches, caramelised onions,
herbs, and a dash of something that no one could ever quite place.

It was a dish that customers returned for time and time again,

and each time they took their first bite,
Brent could see the look of contentment
spread across their faces.
There was something about it, a richness,
a depth of flavour,
that seemed to transport them to another place,
another time.
For Brent, it was more than just a dish.
It was a connection to his grandmother,
to everything she had taught him about the importance of family,
tradition,
and the care that went into every meal
but it also captured the more difficult and dark times of his life.

Despite its popularity, there were times when the Burgundy Stew
began to feel like a burden.
It was a signature dish, yes, but it was also a heavy responsibility.
Every day, Brent poured his heart into preparing it,
and every night he left the kitchen with a sense of exhaustion.
The weight of the stew's importance hung over him,
a constant reminder
that his reputation was tied to this one dish.
He couldn't afford to let it slip,
couldn't afford to let anyone else take over.

As time went on, the pressure of maintaining
the perfection of the Burgundy Stew
began to take its toll.
Brent found himself spending more
and more time in the kitchen,
working late into the night to ensure
that every batch of stew was as perfect as the last.
The other chefs in the kitchen,

Marco included, noticed his increasing isolation.
He was no longer as involved in the
day-to-day operations of the restaurant.
He was consumed by the Burgundy Stew,
and it was starting to affect
his interactions with the rest of the team.

One evening, after the restaurant had closed
and the kitchen was quiet,
Marco approached Brent.
He had seen the strain on Brent's face lately,
and had noticed how the chef had been staying longer
and longer to prepare the stew,
sometimes even locking himself in the kitchen for hours
after the last customer had left.

"Brent," Marco began cautiously, "I think we need to talk."
Brent, who had been busy washing a pot, glanced up. "About what?"
"It's about the Burgundy Stew," Marco said,
his voice gentle but firm.
"You've been making it for years, and it's your signature dish.
But you're wearing yourself thin.
You've been staying late every night to make it,
and it's starting to take a toll on you.
We're all here to help. I know you want it to be perfect,
but you don't have to do it alone.
We can take some of the burden off your shoulders."
Brent's heart tightened. He had been expecting this conversation
but hearing it out loud made it more real.
He looked at Marco, his loyal head chef,
who had worked tirelessly for years to make the restaurant a success.
Marco wasn't just an employee, he was a friend,
someone Brent had come to rely on.

Yet still, the thought of anyone else touching
his Burgundy Stew made him uneasy.

"I appreciate what you're saying, Marco,"
Brent replied, his voice strained.
"But this dish... it's more than just food to me.
It's... it's a connection to my life.
I can't let anyone else make it.
Not yet. Not until I'm sure they understand it the way I do."
Marco nodded, though Brent could see the concern in his eyes.
"I get that. I do. But you've built something incredible here,
Brent. *Eleanor's* is your legacy, and it's a team effort.
You don't have to carry it all by yourself.
You've got people who care about this place
as much as you do."

Brent sighed, the weight of Marco's words settling
on his shoulders.
He knew he was being stubborn,
knew that he couldn't keep going on like this forever.
But letting go of the Burgundy Stew,
letting someone else take over something
that felt so intrinsically tied to his own identity,
was terrifying.
What if it wasn't the same?
What if the dish lost its magic?

"I don't know if I'm ready," Brent said quietly.
"But... I'll think about it."
For the first time in a long while,
Brent allowed himself to think beyond the Burgundy Stew.
He thought about the restaurant,
about the people who had helped him build it,

and about the future.
He realised that he couldn't keep holding on to the past forever.
The next day, Brent sat down with Marco
and the rest of the kitchen team.
He explained his feelings about the Burgundy Stew,
about why it meant so much to him,
and about the difficulty of letting go.
To his surprise, everyone understood.
They respected his connection to the dish.
There was an agreement that Brent would continue
to prepare the dish,
as he had been doing for several years.

CHAPTER TEN

Mother

It had been a long day at the restaurant.
The dinner service had gone smoothly, the kitchen was clean,
and Brent had finished his shift later than usual,
feeling the familiar ache in his feet and the exhaustion
settling into his bones.
The quiet hum of his car engine as he drove
through the streets felt
almost comforting in the stillness of the night.
The usual routine of his post-work drive home
was something Brent had grown accustomed to,
a time to reflect on the day,
to wind down, or simply to allow his thoughts to drift.
But that night, something unexpected happened,
something that would change the course of his life once again.

As Brent pulled into the driveway of his home,
he noticed something out of place.
The porch light was on, but the house was still and silent,
an unusual contrast to the evening's typical quiet.
For a moment, he thought nothing of it,
perhaps the neighbour was visiting,
or a delivery had been left on the doorstep.

But as he turned off the engine and stepped out of the car,
he saw her. Standing by the front door,
her silhouette framed by the dim light, was his mother.
Brent froze for a moment, his heart skipping a beat.
It had been years, too many years.
The last time he'd seen her he was still in school.
His mother, once a familiar presence in his life,
had slipped into the distant corners of his memories,
a figure tied to a painful past.
His mother was standing there,
looking more fragile than he ever remembered.
Her face was thinner, the skin around her eyes
creased with deep lines.
Her posture was slightly hunched,
as though the weight of the years
had caught up to her all at once.
The woman who had once been vibrant and full of life
now seemed to be a shell of that person,
a version of herself worn down by time, hardship, and loss.

For a moment, neither of them spoke.
Brent simply stood there,
unsure of what to say.
So much had happened since they had last seen each other.
So much had changed.
"Mom?" he finally said, his voice soft with surprise.
She looked up at him, her tired eyes searching
his face for recognition.
A faint smile tugged at the corner of her lips,
but it was tinged with sadness.
"Brent," she murmured, her voice thick with emotion.
"I wasn't sure if you'd be home tonight."

Brent took a step toward her, his mind racing.
What was she doing here? Why had she come?
He hadn't expected this.
The years of silence between them weighed heavily in the air,
but despite the years of distance,
the bond between mother and son hadn't completely eroded.
There was a tug in his chest, a pull that couldn't be ignored.
He reached out,
offering her a hand,
and she accepted it hesitantly.
"Come inside," Brent said, his voice more confident
now that the initial shock had worn off.
"We have a lot to catch up on."

His mother stepped inside, her movements slow and measured,
as if she was still unsure of where she belonged.
Brent led her into the living room, where they both took a seat,
the silence hanging between them like a delicate thread.
For a few moments, neither of them spoke.
Brent found himself studying her
more intently than he ever had before.
She seemed so different now,
so much older than the woman he remembered.
Life had undoubtedly taken its toll on her,
just as it had on him in different ways.
Finally, it was his mother who broke the silence.
"I'm sorry, Brent. For everything. For how things turned out...
for everything I did. I know it's too late for apologies,
but I have to say it."
Her voice cracked, and the pain in her words was palpable.
Brent's heart ached for her.
He had spent so many years resenting her
for the choices she had made,

for the things she had allowed to happen in their home
when he was growing up.
His father's violent temper,
the shouting matches,
the broken promises,
those were all memories that had haunted Brent's youth,
shaping him to some extent into the man he had become.
And yet, despite all of that,
 there was still a part of him that longed
for the connection that they once shared.

"It's not too late, Mom," he said gently.
"But I need to understand. I need to know what happened."
His mother looked down at her hands,
the fingers trembling slightly as she wrung them together.
It was clear she had been carrying something heavy for a long time.
"It's hard to explain," she began,
her voice steady but filled with sadness.
"After I sent you to live with Grandma,
things only got worse with your father.
I was right to send you away when I did,
he... he was never a good man, Brent.
Your father and I got back together, and I stayed.
I stayed because I didn't know what else to do.
And then one day... one day, it all went too far.
" She stopped, her eyes clouded with painful memories.
"He killed someone. A man from work.
A disagreement, a fight that ended in murder."
Brent's stomach turned. His father, still the same,
still as unpredictable and dangerous as ever.
Brent had hoped, over the years, that the man would change,
that time would soften him.
But hearing this, hearing what his father had done,

shattered any remaining illusions.

"I don't know what happened to him," his mother continued,
her voice barely above a whisper.
"But he's in prison now. He's been there for several years.
I... I couldn't live with that anymore.
I couldn't live with the shame of what he did
and what he had become.
And I couldn't live alone, not anymore."
She looked at him with pleading eyes. "Brent, I need a place to stay.
I have nowhere else to go."
The words stung.
The truth of what his mother had endured,
and the way she had stayed for so long in a toxic
and dangerous relationship,
was hard for him to fully comprehend.
But at the same time, he understood.
He understood the weight of fear, of uncertainty,
and of the strange ties that kept people from breaking free.
"You're welcome to stay here," Brent said, his voice firm but soft.
"This is your home, too.
You don't have to go anywhere else."
His mother's eyes welled with tears, and she nodded gratefully.
 "I don't deserve your kindness,
Brent. But I'm so thankful."
Brent reached over and placed a hand on her shoulder,
offering her a small, reassuring smile.
"You're my mother, and this is where you belong.
We'll figure it out, one step at a time."

It wasn't going to be easy, Brent knew that.
The years of bitterness and anger wouldn't disappear overnight.
There were still so many things left unsaid,

so many questions left unanswered.
But in that moment, sitting there with his mother,
Brent felt a sense of peace,
a sense of understanding that had been missing for so long.
As they continued to talk that evening,
they caught up on the small details of each other's lives,
the years they had spent apart.
Brent learned that his mother had moved around a lot
after the arrest of his father,
never staying in one place for too long,
always trying to escape the ghosts of her past.
She had tried to build a life for herself, but it had been a struggle.
The years of being trapped in an abusive marriage
had left her with little to show for it.
And yet, she had always carried the memory of him,
her son, with her.
It was the one thing that had kept her going.
"I'm here now, Brent," she said quietly.
"And I won't leave again. Not this time."

There was still so much healing to be done,
so many wounds to mend.
But for the first time in years,
Brent felt like he wasn't alone.
His mother's return wasn't the closure he had imagined,
but it was something else, a new beginning,
a chance to rebuild the relationship they had lost.
And for that, he was grateful.
As the night ended, Brent made up the guest room for his mother,
offering her a place to rest.
And as he sat down on the couch, the familiar sounds of the house,
a creak in the floorboards,
the soft murmur of the wind outside felt different now.

There was a quietness in the air,
but it wasn't the emptiness he had once felt.
It was a new chapter, one that Brent wasn't sure he was ready for,
but one that he was willing to face.

CHAPTER ELEVEN

Ingredients

For years, the neighbourhood had been a picture
of peaceful suburban life.
The streets were lined with well-kept homes,
families gathered at the local park, and the community felt safe.
It was the kind of place where you could leave
your front door unlocked at night
and walk down the street without fear.
Crime was almost unheard of,
and the residents were proud of the security
and stability they had built in their little corner of the world.
But the disappearances had begun a few years back.
It started with a few odd reports.
A neighbour hadn't returned home after an evening walk,
a woman was last seen leaving the grocery store
and never made it back,
and then more names were added to the list.
Soon, it became clear that something dark was happening,
and it was happening close to home.

The local police were initially puzzled.
There were no signs of forced entry into homes,
no witnesses, and no immediate leads.
All the missing people seemed to have vanished without a trace.

In the early days of the investigation,
it was easy to dismiss it as a fluke or a series of isolated incidents.
But as the weeks turned into months,
the disappearances grew in number,
and the mystery deepened.

Residents began to grow uneasy. The once-quiet streets,
so filled with laughter and chatter, now felt empty and ominous.
People started locking their doors earlier in the evening,
and the parks that had once been filled with children playing
became desolate after dark.
There was a palpable tension in the air,
an undercurrent of fear that no one could ignore.

The police, despite their best efforts,
were no closer to finding the cause.
They spent months gathering eyewitness accounts,
conducting door-to-door searches,
and scouring the area for any trace of the missing individuals.
But the only thing they found were personal belongings,
purses, wallets, cell phones,
discarded in alleyways or left in the middle of the street,
as though the people who owned them had simply
vanished into thin air.

Then, an unexpected break in the case came.
One evening, a concerned resident called in to report
something unusual.
The caller claimed to have seen a man behaving
strangely near the local restaurant,
a place that, until then,
had been a fixture of the neighbourhood,
beloved for its food and atmosphere.

The man was described as standing
outside the restaurant late at night,
looking around as if he were waiting for someone.
When questioned, the restaurant's staff knew
nothing about anybody lurking at the restaurant.

The lead seemed insignificant at first,
but it sparked an idea in one of the detectives.
The restaurant had always been a bit of a mystery to outsiders.
The owner, Brent Pineridge,
had built a reputation for being a private man,
one who rarely socialised outside of the confines of his business.
While his culinary talents were unquestionable,
there was something unsettling about how little
he shared with the people around him.
His signature dish, the Burgundy stew, was legendary,
a rich, hearty meal that had a taste unlike anything else.
People came from miles around just to try it,
and they returned time and time again,
unable to resist its unique flavour.

The detective couldn't shake the nagging feeling
that there might be a connection
between the restaurant and the disappearances.
There was no solid evidence, only the lingering suspicion
that something wasn't quite right.
The police launched a covert operation,
assigning undercover officers to frequent the restaurant,
hoping to observe anything that might lead them to the truth.

As the months passed, the officers became more
and more entrenched
in the daily operations of the restaurant.

They observed the staff, listened to conversations,
and quietly took note of every detail.
It wasn't long before they started to uncover a series
of strange coincidences,
all pointing back to the same man:
Brent Pineridge.

Brent was meticulous. His staff adored him for his leadership,
and he had built a strong, loyal team.
But there was one thing that seemed increasingly out of place:
his absolute secrecy
surrounding the preparation of his signature dish.
The Burgundy stew was a well-loved part of the restaurant's menu,
but no one, not even his most trusted chefs,
knew exactly what went into it.
Brent was the only one who prepared it,
and he never allowed anyone else to assist.
This was a fact that had always raised eyebrows,
but it was brushed off as simply the eccentricity of a chef
at the top of his game.
The undercover officers, however, had no time for eccentricity.
They were trained to notice things others might miss,
and they noticed an unsettling pattern.
The same customers who had come into the restaurant
on multiple occasions were also sometimes the ones
who went missing after some time.
It was a small detail, but it was enough to set off alarm bells.

In the weeks that followed, the investigation uncovered
even more disturbing evidence.
Personal items belonging to the missing persons
were found in the restaurant's kitchen,
hidden in plain sight.

A purse here, a wallet there. Items that had been reported
as belonging to the missing.

But it was when the undercover police found a
hidden storage room in the basement of the restaurant
that the truth finally began to come to light.
When the police had enough evidence, they moved swiftly.
They raided the restaurant in the dead of night
with a search warrant,
catching Brent off guard as he was preparing
yet another batch of the Burgundy stew.
He didn't resist as they arrested him,
 but the shock of the truth was written all over his face.
He had never expected to be caught,
not after all these years of carefully hiding his secret.
But the truth always comes out in the end.

When the police gained access and searched
the storage room they found that it was cold and sterile,
and it held nothing of the kind of ingredients
you might expect in a kitchen.
There were no fresh herbs or vegetables,
no pots or pans. Instead,
there were carefully labelled jars,
each containing a different part of human anatomy
—organs, flesh, and bone.

The officers were horrified as they pieced together
what had been happening right under their noses.
Brent Pineridge had been abducting vulnerable individuals
from around the neighbourhood.
He had used the restaurant's facilities to butcher their bodies,
carefully preparing specific cuts of meat that he then marinated

and incorporated into his Burgundy stew.

The recipe that had become so beloved,
so highly praised by customers,
was a horrifying blend of human flesh.
Brent Pineridge had been killing and cooking people,
using the restaurant as his private butchery.
Each victim had been carefully chosen
—usually someone who was alone and vulnerable.
They had been abducted in the dead of night,
killed, and then processed in the restaurant's kitchen,
where they became part of the dish
that kept the customers coming back for more.

The trial that followed was one of the most horrific
in the town's history.
The details of how each victim had been lured to their death,
butchered, and turned into a dish that had been
served to many unsuspecting customers
was almost too much to bear.
The once-celebrated restaurant became a symbol of horror,
and the people who had once raved about the Burgundy stew,
they were left with a profound sense of guilt and disgust
that would haunt them for the rest of their lives.

Brent Pineridge was convicted of multiple murders
and sentenced to life in prison.
He never showed any remorse for his actions,
and the public was left to grapple with the realisation that someone
they had trusted had been hiding such a monstrous secret.
He spent the rest of his life behind bars,
dying of natural causes in his prison cell.
But the legacy of his crimes would linger long after his death.

The neighbourhood would never be the same,
and neither would the people who had once dined at his restaurant.

CHAPTER TWELVE

Epilogue/Conclusion

Years passed, but the shadows of Brent Pineridge's deeds
lingered like a dark stain on the community.
The restaurant, once a beacon of culinary excellence,
was abandoned and eventually demolished,
its land left barren as if the earth itself refused to bear its weight.

Locals avoided the area, whispering tales
of ghostly cries in the night
and phantom aromas of Burgundy stew wafting through the air.
The families of the victims tried to rebuild their lives,
but the scars ran deep.
Support groups formed,
offering solace to those who had lost loved ones
or who had unknowingly consumed the unspeakable.
Therapy sessions became a common refuge for those grappling
with the grotesque truth,
that something as simple as a meal had made them
unwitting participants in the horror.

The trial became a grim case study, dissected by criminologists
and psychologists seeking to understand how
Brent Pineridge, a man once lauded as a talented chef,
could have concealed such malevolence.

Documentaries, books, and podcasts emerged,
each exploring the macabre tale,
ensuring that the story of the "Burgundy Butcher"
would not fade into obscurity.

But for those who had lived through it,
no amount of analysis or explanation could undo the trauma.
The town remained haunted by the knowledge
of what had transpired,
and an unspoken pact arose among its residents,
they would never let their guard down again.

Though Brent Pineridge was gone,
his dark legacy served as a stark reminder of the fragility of trust
and the depths of human depravity.
And so, the town moved forward, not unscathed, but resolute,
determined to honour the lives lost and to ensure
that such horrors would never take root again.